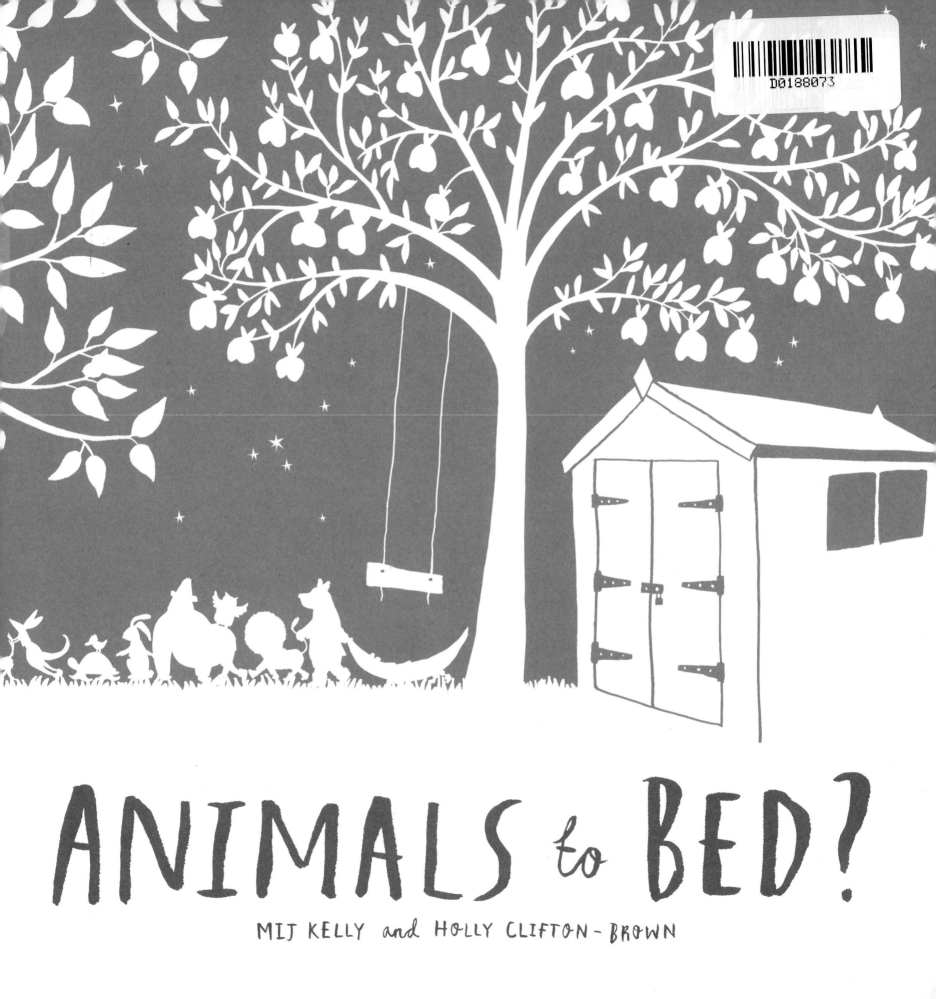

ANIMALS to BED?

MIJ KELLY and HOLLY CLIFTON-BROWN

At the end of the day,
at the start of the night,
when the earth is half dark,
when the sky is half light,

who puts the
animals to bed?

Who helps the cat
down from the shed?

Who finds the bear
that went astray
and quiets the dog
that wants to play?

Who picks the downy duckling up

and soothes the yawning sea-lion pup?

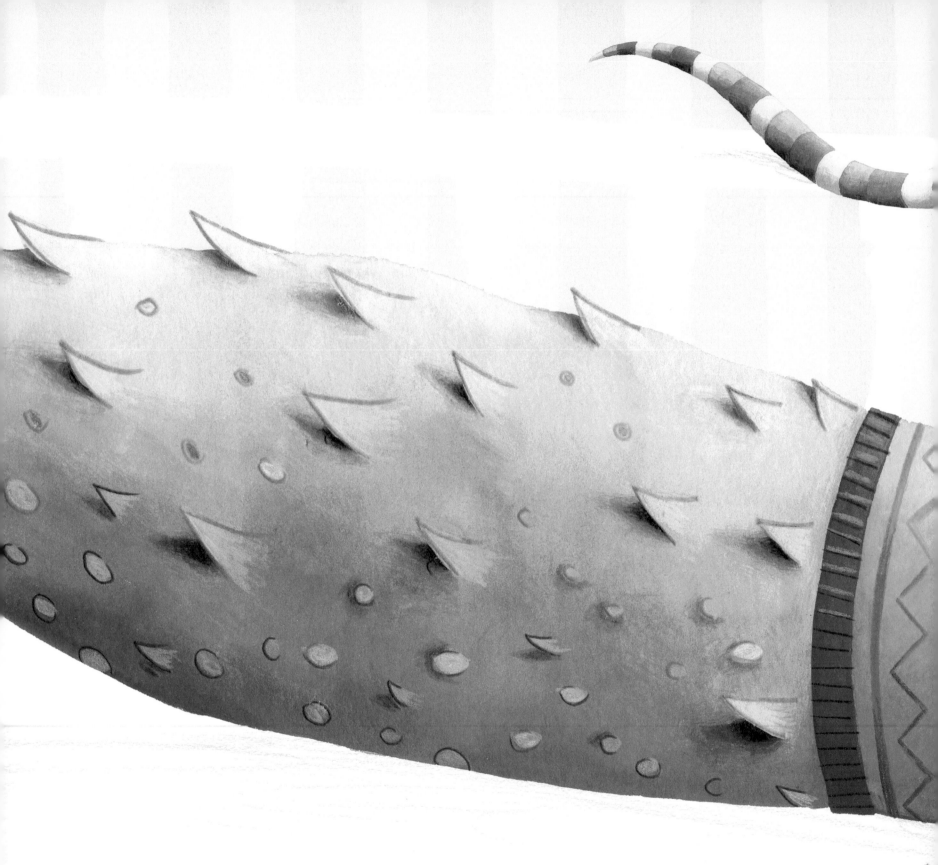

Who blows the crocodile a kiss

and asks the snake - please - not to hiss,

tells elephant
to close his eyes,

and sings the lion a lullaby?

When tawny owl goes:

"Twit-too-woo,"

who whispers:
"Hush?"

Oh tell me who
strokes the tired
old tiger's head?
Who puts the
animals to bed?

Is it you? Is it you?
Well, snuggle down too,

with your lion and your
bear, or your kangaroo,

with rabbit and monkey,
penguin and dog,
gorilla and turtle,
or maybe with frog.

Give them all a big hug
and turn down the light

and with the whole wide, wild world
sleep in peace for the night.